My Brother's Ghost

ALLAN AHLBERG

VIKING

VIKING

Published by the Penguin Group
Penguin Putnam Books for Young Readers,
345 Hudson Street, New York, New York 10014, U.S.A.
Penguin Books Ltd, 27 Wrights Lane, London W8 5TZ, England
Penguin Books Australia Ltd, Ringwood, Victoria, Australia
Penguin Books Canada Ltd, 10 Alcorn Avenue, Toronto, Ontario, Canada M4V 3B2
Penguin Books (N.Z.) Ltd, 182-190 Wairau Road, Auckland 10, New Zealand

Penguin Books Ltd, Registered Offices: Harmondsworth, Middlesex, England
First published in Great Britain in 2000 by Viking.

Published in the U.S.A. in 2001 by Viking,
a division of Penguin Putnam Books for Young Readers.

1 3 5 7 9 10 8 6 4 2

LIBRARY OF CONGRESS CATALOGING-IN-PUBLICATION DATA
Ahlberg, Allan.
My brother's ghost / Allan Ahlberg.
p.   cm.
Summary: Orphaned by the death of their parents and bereft by the sudden
death of their older brother Tom, nine-year-old Frances and three-year-old Henry
are comforted by Tom's ghost, who helps them in difficult situations at home
with their aunt and uncle and at school.
ISBN 0-670-89290-4
[1. Ghosts—Fiction. 2. Death—Fiction. 3. Brothers and sisters—Fiction.
4. Orphans—Fiction. 5. Aunts—Fiction. 6. England—Fiction.] I. Title.
PZ7.A2688 Msf 2001 [Fic]—dc21 00-047739

Printed in Great Britain
Set in Cochin

For Jessica

Contents

What I am about to tell you is true, well, as true as I can make it. (These things happened forty years ago.) Nothing is made up. Where I could not remember the details, I have left them out.

My name is Frances Fogarty. I am the middle child, the sister, in the story. Tom was my brother. Harry was, and happily still is, my brother. Marge was my aunt, Rufus my dog, Rosalind my enemy. And so on.

You won't, I don't suppose, believe in ghosts. That can't be helped. The truth is, in a curious way I'm not sure I do either. Ghosts? I cannot speak for ghosts in general, numbers of ghosts. No . . . just the one.

The Funeral

H E WAS TEN WHEN it happened, and I was nine and Harry was three. Running out into the street after Rufus, he was hit by nothing more than a silent, gliding milk-float. His head cracked down against the pavement edge. A fleck of blood rose up between his lips. His legs shook briefly, one heel rattling like a drumstick against the side of the float. And then he died.

My brother, my clever, understanding older brother. My best friend and biggest pest of course sometimes. The sharer of my secrets, the buffer between me and Harry. Dead.

The milkman I remember was in tears, smashed bottles at his feet, milk running in the gutter. I had hold of Harry's hand. Rufus, all unconcerned, was still prancing about.

Four days later, the funeral. A pair of black cars, men in black suits, flowers and wreaths, the vicar. Harry and I were there. Uncle Stan said we should stay home. Auntie Marge said we should go. So we went.

It was a morning funeral. The grass in the cemetery was still wet with dew. The vicar spoke and the coffin was lowered on ropes into the ground. I remember then a train went by – invisibly in the cutting – the hiss and rattle of it, steam rising.

Who else was there besides us and Uncle Stan and Auntie Marge? The vicar, I've mentioned him. The under-taker's men. The grave diggers waiting at a distance. A neighbour, a friend of Auntie Marge's, had come I think, and the woman who ran the Cubs. The milk-man too, perhaps. Somebody from the school.

And it was cold, I remember that, the low November sunlight glittering on the wet headstones. There was the sound of traffic from the road, the rumble of the presses in the nearby Creda factory.

It was Harry who saw him first. He grabbed my sleeve but said nothing. I looked . . . and there was Tom. He had his hands in his pockets, his jacket collar up. His hair was as uncombed, as wild as ever. And he was leaning against a tree.

Looking for Tom

W E'D HAD OUR SHARE of troubles when Tom was alive. They did not go away after he died. Auntie Marge was softer with us for a day or two following the funeral. A bit of extra cake at teatime; a couple of comics at the weekend; now and then asking us how we were. But Harry was still wetting the bed, and soon she was yelling at him again as loud as ever and slapping the backs of his little legs. And I was yelling at her and getting clouted too. And Uncle Stan was sloping off embarrassed to his shed. Things were back to normal.

Except of course for Tom.

We *had* seen him. At least Harry and I had. As we left the cemetery we had walked right past the tree where he was leaning. It was his face as clear as day. He looked at us, frowning, puzzled perhaps, as though our presence was a surprise to *him*. A little later, as the car drove away at a snail's pace, I saw him again, standing beside the grave. The grave diggers had removed the carpets of artificial grass, the platform of planks, and were shovelling the soil back into the hole. Tom was watching them.

School was hateful to me. I couldn't join in with things because of my leg. (Polio, I wore a caliper.) My teacher, Mrs Harris, said I was a scowler. (I was!) Rosalind and her gang were much of the time unfriendly, or worse. All the same, the day after the funeral I was back, only this time with no Tom to walk with or look out for me in the playground. Again, just as with Auntie Marge, there was a day or two of sympathetic smiles and considerate voices – Maureen Copper even shared her liquorice with me – before things got back to normal.

On Saturday I went looking for Tom.

I had some errands to do for Auntie Marge in the morning. There was a steady drizzling rain in the early afternoon. So it was nearly four o'clock when I left the house. Rufus was with me, my excuse for going out.

The cemetery was divided into two parts, with a road, Cemetery Road, passing between them. I stood at the gates just after four. More rain was threatening. Already the street lights were beginning to glow. Rufus tugged us in. There was a light shining out from the side door of the chapel, I remember. Three or four people with flowers and cans of water were moving about. There was a smell of chrysanthemums.

What must I have been thinking then, as I stepped off down the path? I was only nine, after all. The cemetery was a place of morbid fears and dread. A place you avoided. A place you *ran* past (if you could).

Tom. I was thinking of Tom. I was scared and thinking of Tom. Holding Rufus close in on his lead for comfort and looking for Tom. Tom was here. He was here. *How* was he here?

The tree first, dripping noisily on its own dead leaves. No Tom. Then the grave: a mound of earth – drenched wreaths and flowers – smudgy, unreadable messages on little cards – muddy footprints in the grass. No Tom.

It was drizzling again now. My leg had begun to ache, the cold metal of the caliper chafing against my knee. Rufus was kicking his back legs in the loose soil. I turned and came away.

On Cemetery Road the street lights shone in the damp air, smudgily, like the blurry messages on the little cards. The air itself had a yellow, sulphurous tinge. (There were more coal fires and factory chimneys in those days.) A fog was beginning to form.

At the end of our street I let Rufus off his lead. He liked to run, to *hurtle* really, home from there. I limped on up to the house. On the low wall at the front enclosing a tiny patch of garden, Tom was sitting. His face still had that puzzled frowning look. His collar was still up.

I stood, my hair soaking wet and flat against my head, drops of water on my nose and ears and chin. Tom's mouth was open. He was speaking or trying to, it seemed. There was no sound, as though a sheet of glass was placed between us. He made a gesture with his hand, a wave perhaps. There was a sharp tapping at the window. Auntie Marge was scowling at me, she was a scowler too. She wondered at me standing so still in the rain, wanted me in for my tea.

Tom watched me as I limped off down

the entry. *His* hair, I just had time to notice, was bone dry.

Rufus

THAT NIGHT I TRIED to talk to Harry. I told him about Tom. That I had seen him again, here at the house. That Auntie Marge had not seen him. That when I got to the window straight after tea, he was no longer there. Harry said little. He wasn't talking much in those days anyway. 'No, no!' when Marge came after him. 'Milk,' sometimes to me at breakfast. And now, 'Tom – see Tom.'

Harry's life I think at that time had just curled up into a ball. He was somewhere inside, sitting it out.

As soon as Harry was asleep, I crept out onto the landing and into Tom's room. Auntie Marge and Uncle Stan were downstairs with the radio on. Yellow foggy light from the street lamp lit up two thirds of the room and cast the rest into shadow. I stood uncertainly beside Tom's narrow bed. His things were all around me: Meccano models, balsa wood planes, his green Cubs' jumper with badges down the sleeves, marbles, cigarette cards . . . shoes. I sat on the bed and felt like an intruder.

I shivered. Already Tom's room was

colder than the rest of the house and had begun to acquire that musty, unlived-in smell. A double-decker bus went sailing past the window. I sat there with my hands in my lap. Then the shapes in the room dissolved, and I began to cry.

The next day, Sunday, Harry and I went to Sunday school. We sang 'Ye Holy Angels Bright' and did a Bible quiz. I spent our collection money in Starkey's Sweet Shop. When we got home Auntie Marge smelled the sherbet on us, gave me a clout and sent the pair of us to our room. No tea, she said. No toys. Not a sound. Uncle Stan came in later, sheepishly, with a couple of biscuits. (Of course next morning she found the crumbs and *he* got a telling off.) The afternoon passed. It became darker in the room. (No light on.) Harry dozed off on his bed. I stood for a while at the window staring down into the yard. Presently, out came Rufus snuffling around, looking for amusement. I watched, and suddenly there was Tom. He was following Rufus here and there across the yard. Rufus had hold of an old deflated ball and was shaking it like a rat. Tom held out a hand, crouched down beside him, attempted to ruffle his furry neck. And Rufus, dim *un*seeing Rufus, no sixth sense (hardly five), went bounding through him.

Bad Times

I WILL SAY SOMETHING here about polio. It is not, after all and thank goodness, a disease that any of us has cause to fear these days. But in those days ... well, there were two others in my school with calipers on their legs. There was also a boy, I seem to remember, who had it and was so ill he just stayed home.

Polio – poliomyelitis – is a virus. One

of its many unpleasant effects is to paralyse certain muscles. You needed then to wear a metal and leather brace, a 'caliper' as it was called. This helped your weakened leg (or legs) to support your weight. I had caught polio when I was six and had been wearing a caliper for about a year and a half.

Rosalind Phipps was just a nasty child, I can see this now. Though maybe she had her troubles too. (What went on in *her* house, I wonder.) She was a bully to me, she and her spiteful gang. 'Frances Frogarty,' they would chant in their sarcastic sing-song voices. It drove me crazy. I had a temper. I would rise to the bait and Rosalind knew it. Then having got me all worked up she would somehow cunningly duck out of sight, leaving me to suffer the consequences with Mrs Harris, Mr Cork or whoever. Also she would say bad things about Harry (her little sister and Harry went to the same nursery), or worse about our parents. 'You only live with your Auntie!' I wanted to punch her.

So I was having a bad time at school and Harry and I were having a bad time at home. Auntie Marge had no interest in children, no maternal instincts I heard her say on one occasion. When Tom was around he often managed to deflect her anger. Without him we were horribly exposed. She was impatient, humour-less, cruel.

The following week, the week after the funeral, it snowed for the first time. Harry stood in wonder at the bedroom window. 'Snow,' he whispered. He had woken me up to see it. My enthusiasm was less than his. I was thinking more of the ice that would surely follow, the slippery pavements, my clumsy leg.

At eight o'clock in came Marge in her blackest mood. She threw the blankets back from Harry's bed, wrinkled her nose and yelled. (He was on my bed already, behind me.) 'I'm sick of this!' She snatched the wet sheet from the bed and the rubber sheet beneath and hurled them to the floor. 'Sick, sick, sick!'

Two nights later I woke in the half light, the curtains partly open, a clear sky, a moon, light bouncing up from the frosty snow. Harry was stumbling out of bed, feeling his way with Tom beside him. They left the room. I followed. The lino beneath my feet was freezing. The clock downstairs struck twice. I could hear Rufus groaning in his sleep.

I found Harry in the bathroom, his pyjama trousers around his feet, having a sleepwalking wee. Tom was there. Somehow I knew better than to interfere. Tom glanced at me over his shoulder. He had a hand on Harry's shoulder. (Could Harry feel it?)

I left. Minutes later Harry came back to bed, his eyes half shut, alone. I fell asleep then and dreamt my usual dream or one of them. Mum and I were at the seaside tucking our dresses into our knickers, splashing in the waves. Dad was in the distance . . . calling.

The next night Tom came again, and the next and the next. He arrived at different times: twelve-thirty, two o'clock, three. He got Harry up, or Harry got himself up, and led him to the bathroom. Each night Harry had a wee. Each morning Harry's bed was dry.

I struggled to make sense of what was

happening. Tom was taking Harry to the toilet. How did he accomplish this? Could Harry feel Tom's hand upon his shoulder? (Rufus after all had leapt straight through him.) Could Tom *communicate* with Harry? Was Harry hearing more than I was? For I was hearing nothing, not a sound. On that second night, for instance, Tom returned to the bedroom and stood at the window. The moonlight caught his springy tousled hair. His collar was still up. Harry had dropped straight back into sleep. I sat up in bed and called Tom's name, an urgent whisper. 'Tom? Tom!' He turned to face me. Once more his mouth was open. He spoke, or tried to. Once more the plate of glass between us. No sound.

But the next night there was a sound, though one I'd rather not have heard. It was a slow growling sound, like something played at the wrong speed. 'Frr.' For the first time, I remember, I was really afraid. I pulled the bedclothes over my head and held my breath. 'Frr.' When I peeped out later, Tom was gone.

The thing is, it was Tom who was making this awful noise, all the while with a serious, almost hopeful look in his eyes as though he expected *me* to understand it. Well, I believe I may have sensed something then or begun to. It *was* my brother I was hearing, seeing –

yes of course my brother, my loving brother, my graceful, quiet, clever brother. But then again, not quite my brother now. It was my brother's ghost.

The Fight

IT'S OCCURRED TO ME (just now, as I write) that really so far I have not described exactly what it was that Harry and I *saw* when we saw Tom. The main thing is, you see, Tom was never transparent or wispy like the ghosts you sometimes get in the movies. He was no apparition. You might walk through him, but you couldn't see through him. (At least, we couldn't. Others it seems couldn't see him at all.) So you could say the way he looked to us was completely normal. The only exception to this was sudden movement, quick changes of direction. At such times Tom's outline, the edges of him, would quiver and blur like a swimmer under water or someone seen in the distance through a heat haze.

Mrs Harris was an average sort of teacher. She did her best for me, I suppose, though I was not among her favourites. I was a prickly child altogether. I had no winning ways. Consequently, when the fight happened it was hardly a surprise to me when Mrs

Harris took the wrong side, blamed the wrong person.

It was December now, Christmas and my birthday approaching. We decorated the classroom with silver paper chains and cotton wool snowmen. Mrs Harris brought some twigs of holly from her own garden. We made cards for our mums and dads, or, added Mrs Harris hastily, our grandmas, cousins, aunties – anybody really. I made mine for Harry.

In the last week of the term we had a Christmas dinner in the hall. Some of the teachers joined in wearing party hats. Bad luck brought me to Rosalind's table.

I was not in the best of moods to begin with. Auntie Marge had had a go at us that morning about something or other. Tom had not been near us for two or three days. My leg was aching. So whatever it was that Rosalind said or did – it was something – I was ready for her. I pushed her off her chair. A bowl of Christmas pudding and custard followed her to the floor. She aimed a sly kick at me, and I fell on her.

There was a satisfying whoosh of air from Rosalind. My heavy calipered leg was a help too on this occasion. I would surely have punched my enemy then. I would have bitten her. But Mrs Harris in her crooked party hat dragged me away.

❉

The following morning Tom walked with me to school. On the way, at the corner of Seymour Road and Tugg Street, he completed his first spoken word. 'Frr . . . ances,' he said.

Remembering

MY MEMORIES OF WHAT happened to us all those years ago are unreliable at times, obliterated even. But I remember that first walk with Tom completely. Every detail. It's like a film in my head.

I remember the glistening blue-brick pavement, the rusty railings and the ivy outside the Rolfe Street Baptist Chapel, the belching smoke from one of old man

Cutler's allotment bonfires. I remember him too, in his off-white painter's overalls and his pork pie hat, poking at it. I remember colliding with Herbie, the bread man, in the first shock of seeing Tom. I remember the pleasure and relief in Tom's face when he got that first word – my name! – out. Above all, though, I remember my feelings.

I felt so happy and sad ... and strange. Tom just appeared, you see. (I nearly said, 'out of nowhere'.) He spoke, only the one word. And then he simply walked beside me as he had ever used to.

What a curious experience, to walk to school with a ghost. How odd I must have seemed, glancing sideways, dodging unnecessarily, smiling into the thin air. I was looking out for Tom. It distressed me when someone went blundering through him. But he – out of habit? – was avoiding them anyway. So it rarely happened. I felt no urge to talk yet, to interrogate him. (Where had he been?) Mainly, I believe, I was just so glad of his company. Going to school with Tom, entering the playground with Tom, merely knowing he was present in the building, had always helped me in the past. It was helping me now.

Tom and I joined the cluster of parents and children at the school crossing. I studied Tom out of the corner of my eye. He was studying me. Both of us smiled. It came into my mind then how strange all of this must be for *him*. And then I had another thought: *he was working it out.*

Years before, back in the days when we were a family, I recall Tom brought a maths book home. He was clever at maths, could do most of it in his head and simply put the answers down. Anyway, on this occasion his teacher had written in the margin next to an especially complicated sum that Tom had got right, 'How did you get this answer?' And Tom in the tiniest writing had replied:

'I worked it out!'

This became a joke in our family for quite a while, a catchphrase even. How did you . . .? I worked it out.

The school bell was ringing. Mr Hawkins was out on the forecourt shovelling coke down the chute into his boiler room. Tom stopped to watch. Rosalind, Amanda and the others were hanging around at the school gates. I observed a satisfying-looking bruise on Rosalind's leg, a wary look in her eye. I walked straight past them.

Canada

THE WEEKS AND MONTHS went by, Christmas and my birthday with them. For a while the circumstances of our lives improved. Harry was no longer wetting the bed at all. He had also now begun to talk more, run around more. He played in the yard, when the weather permitted, with a little friend he'd made at the nursery. And I got invited to a party! What sort of party or who invited me, I'm ashamed to say I have forgotten. But I remember the dress. And I remember Auntie Marge taking me out one Saturday morning to Haywoods Outfitters to buy it.

Marge *was* a terror, but not all the time. She had her better side too. She was a hard worker, cleaning other people's houses in the daytime and offices at night. Much of her wages I'm sure were spent on us. Also, although she did yell at us and hit us, she was often truly sorry for it later. She would come up to our room sometimes with tears in her eyes and attempt to cuddle us, offer us little treats.

One more improvement: I had begun

having physiotherapy for my polio-stricken leg, exercises to strengthen the wasted muscle. In time, it was suggested, I might have the caliper removed, stand and walk unaided.

Actually, I have a confession to make about this leg. When I began my story, I had half a mind not to mention it, write myself a pair of normal legs, as it were. It was partly Harry's idea. (He has been reading my manuscript as I write it.) In his opinion the leg is just too much: no mum, no dad, no brother, a wicked auntie and to cap it all a pathetic poor old *limping* leg. Like Tiny Tim. Unbelievable! (according to Harry).

Well, I do want you to believe it of

course, despite what I said at the beginning. And it does seem rather ridiculous now, all those heaped-up troubles (and more to come) – like Job in the Bible. The leg's too much, says Harry. Well, it was too much, I suppose, for me at times. I was hugely sick of it and often wished it gone. But it is a part of the truth, a part of me (Ha!), so I have kept it in.

Meanwhile, what about Tom? Tom came and went. He talked more too, in his new-found gravelly voice – haltingly, long effort-filled pauses, silences. He talked in our room at night, in the park beside me walking Rufus, in the cemetery even on one occasion, with Auntie Marge close by putting flowers on *his* grave. He talked to me, and to Harry sometimes . . . and to Rufus.

Rufus, you see, had really been more Tom's dog than mine. Tom couldn't give up trying to get through to him. I can see him now, crouching beside that little heedless dog or racing after him across the football pitches. Tom made light of his rejections. 'Bad dog . . . Rufus!' he'd say when Rufus ignored him for the umpteenth time. But you could tell he wasn't happy about it. It's an odd thing, but I almost think that watching Tom with Rufus on those occasions was more unbearable than all of it. Tears would come to my eyes and I would feel Tom's loss – my loss of him, his of Rufus. Yes.

Then at the beginning of March, a flurry of events. Auntie Marge scalded her arm slightly in the steam from a boiling pan. Rufus sneaked his way into the front room and attacked the padded seat of one of Marge's favourite chairs, chewed it up almost altogether. And Uncle Stan lost his job.

The lost job was the most significant thing of course, but it was Rufus that triggered the explosion. Marge went berserk. She chased poor Rufus round the kitchen with a broom and then with a clothes line, lashing at him as he cowered under the table. Harry quivered in a corner. Tom stood powerlessly by. I threw a fit.

I rushed at Marge and pushed her violently in the small of the back. (I could not bear the terrible guilt-stricken look in Rufus's eyes.) She toppled sideways and brought a cut glass vase – another favourite – crashing to the floor. She screamed – swore, in fact – and turned on me. I bolted through the kitchen door and ran, Rufus ahead of me.

Things were back again to normal.

That night I lay in bed unable to sleep. Harry was sleeping. Rufus was chained up in the yard below, whining; you could just hear him. Tom was somewhere else.

Eventually I got up and crept onto the landing. A glow of light rising from the rooms below. Voices and clinking cups. Auntie Marge was doing most of the talking. She sounded calm. Stan spoke now and then. I could not make out much of what was said, and yet I felt a sudden clutch of fear. This was the first time, I am fairly sure, that *Canada* was mentioned.

Ghost Talk

THERE IS A WAY in which with time we can take anything for granted. The strange becomes familiar, the extraordinary ordinary. As the year moved on, winter into spring, Tom's involvement with us, his presence in our lives (our presence in his death?) became what we expected, what we were used to. Normal. The mystery and the matter-of-factness were one and the same. We told no one, by the way, not a soul. The secret was ours.

Yet periodically it would come upon me how bewildering, how unfathomably odd it all was. Here was Tom, my dear dead brother, leaning over Harry's bed perhaps, or sitting beside me on a park bench, his eternal jacket collar up, smiling, frowning. And yet if I were just to reach out (which I never did), put my hand upon his arm . . .

How can I convey the strangeness of him? He was so like his previous self, but then . . . There was the rasp and graininess of his new voice, the almost imperceptible peculiarities in his appearance. No motion, no wind in his unruly hair, no rain on his face, only that curious shimmering, shivering at the edges of him when he ran. No actual contact either, with the tree he was supposedly leaning against; the pavement, floor, grass on which he apparently stood. He was here and with us, and elsewhere.

Elsewhere; that was a conundrum too. I came to believe that Tom was like some kind of mobile light bulb, moving himself here and there, switching himself on and off. Except he couldn't always find the switch and had no map. Tom was bewildered too. He compared his condition once to a kind of dreaming. The logic of normal life did not apply.

When he wasn't 'somewhere' – usually that meant with me and Harry – he had no memories at all. Then sometimes, randomly, he'd find himself stood watching a football match on Barnford Hill or boys fishing in the Tipton canal. Once he even got as far as Dudley Zoo; a keeper with his bucket, thrown fish in the air, the glazed and playful seals.

Tom's talk: another conundrum. I wish you could have heard it; the telegram sentences, out-of-step remarks, huge silences. There was not much conversation, that was for sure. He rarely answered questions directly, though something might emerge days or even weeks later. Talking to Tom was a tennis match with few rallies. But at least in time the tension in his speech relaxed, the production of the words themselves was less of a strain. Tom would utter the most perplexing, unconnected thoughts serenely.

Yet consider too what he achieved. Out of his ghostly maze he somehow made his way. He got to Harry when he was needed. And he got to me.

The Thief

IT WAS MAY NOW. Tom had recently seen the seals and over a spread of three or four days told me about them. (Stan surprised me in the kitchen on one of these occasions, talking to myself apparently, and gave me a funny look.) Harry had the measles, Rosalind too incidentally. Rufus was wilder than ever and had got his ear chewed up in a fight. And I was taking sixpences from Marge's Christmas jar.

Stealing. Yes, you would have to say it was. And yet . . . Marge, you see, was strict about most things. Jobs, for instance. You got pocket money but you did jobs for it. Even Harry had jobs. Well, I was doing the jobs and she, quite often, for no reason in my opinion, was stopping my pocket money. So I was paying myself what I was owed, give or take a sixpence.

Stan, though, had no job. He spent much time in his shed, making shelves and a bathroom cabinet. He helped out on a friend's allotment and got paid in cabbages and such. He walked Rufus all over the Rounds Green Hills till even the dog had had enough.

Canada had some connection with Stan's unemployment, I knew that much. Stan had cousins in Toronto. Letters with Canadian stamps would arrive from time to time. But lately there had been a rush of them. Conversations with hints of Canada – Toronto, dollars, cousin Ruth – would fade into silence when I entered the room. One day Uncle Stan (in his best suit) and Auntie Marge took the train to London, leaving us with our neighbour, Shirley. They did not return till after dark. I heard Canada again from my listening post at the top of the stairs.

Then, the inevitable: Marge found out about the sixpences, caught me red-handed in fact. (I looked as guilty as Rufus.) She of course erupted. I was a bad girl, a wicked girl altogether. A little thief. Ungrateful. After all she'd done. She was just sick of me, sick of this whole place – street, town, country! – and would be glad to leave.

Now out it all came. Canada. That was the place, she said, for her and Stan anyway. But not for me, no. No thieves wanted in Canada. I would stay right here (no mention of Harry). 'Yes . . . see if they'll have you in Caldicott Road!'

All this happened one Wednesday afternoon in the half-term holiday. Harry was at his friend's house, Stan out with Rufus. I ended up in my room; Marge was banging around downstairs. I sat on my bed and scowled at the grey, rain-spattered window. I pulled my tin box out from under the bed and opened it. I spread its contents on the floor, took up a bracelet and put it on.

Tom was beside me, kneeling. He stretched out a hand towards a tattered envelope with photographs in it. 'Black,' he said. The rain came rattling harder against the glass. Downstairs I heard a door slam, Rufus barking. 'Pool,' said Tom.

Important Things

'BLACKPOOL,' TOM HAD SAID, and I knew what he wanted. I removed a photograph from the envelope. It was smaller than the rest, black and white. It showed a skinny boy with wet hair in swimming trunks shading his eyes from the sun. Beside him a smaller scowling girl, barefoot in a sundress. On the back was written in our mother's hand:

'Thomas and Frances
Blackpool 1952.'

This battered green tin box was my consolation, Tom's too at times. It contained my important things: a little turquoise bracelet, present from Mum, a Japanese fan that Dad had brought back from his travels, a tiny yellowing paper plane that he had made, a brooch with Grandma's photo in it. And so on. The box itself had belonged to my dad. It had his initials, R.F.F., painted in white letters on the side.

Once there had been four of us, you see. Our dad had been a soldier. He died in the Korean war in 1953. Five months later Mum died giving birth to Harry.

After the funeral we moved down to the Midlands and came to live with Marge and Stan. Yes, once there had been four of us, then three, then briefly four again, then three again . . . now two.

I fell asleep, dozed off on the bed though it was still light outside, Harry not yet back from his friend's. I had the dream again, the familiar simple mystifying dream. We're on the beach. Dad's in the water, swimming, waving. Mum's in a deckchair fast asleep. Tom is missing from the scene. I'm running from a distance, anxious.

Running Away

CANADA WAS BAD NEWS. Caldicott Road was worse. In that town in those days misbehaving children were commonly threatened with two unpleasant possibilities. One was the rag-and-bone man, the other Caldicott Road. Caldicott Road was a children's home. I had *been* in a children's home once before, after Mum died and before Marge and Stan came up to fetch us.

I remembered the experience too well: awful food, lumpy beds, a disinfected unhomely smell, the sense of being abandoned.

It was eight o'clock that same evening. Marge was out cleaning offices. Stan had nipped round to the allotments for half an hour. Harry and I were supposedly in bed.

I packed two bags, one for Harry. I had explained to him that we were going to visit Auntie Annie. Annie was our other auntie, the one we almost never saw. She and Marge weren't speaking. (It's just occurred to me, she would have been at Tom's funeral too. What else have I forgotten?)

Tom appeared as we were getting our coats on, his face serious and frowning. 'Not,' he said. And some time later, 'go!' But we were going anyway. I was worked up, frantic and afraid. Stan might come back at any minute. I was defiant too, another handful of sixpences in my pocket.

'Stay!' said Tom. He was in the hallway now, his arms out wide as though to stop us. We squeezed past him.

Harry and I left the house, left Rufus too, chained up in the yard. (He'd been chewing again.) I could not take Rufus, I needed both hands for the bags and Harry.

Tom pursued us for a time down the street till suddenly he was no longer there. The street lamps had begun to glow. Dark masses of cloud hung in the sky before us. I hurried Harry along. Auntie Annie lived out on the Wolverhampton Road. I thought that we could find our way there, hoped we could. But this journey of course had more to do with leaving than arriving.

In Tugg Street we met Mrs Starkey on the steps of her shop, putting up her umbrella. Spots of rain had begun to fall.

'Hallo, dearies – you're out late!'

Harry started on about Auntie Annie but I kept him moving. The rain fell heavier. We took shelter in the paper shop doorway. Harry was getting restless. For a time we stood just staring out into the glistening empty street. A dog came trotting purposefully along; a man went by on a motorbike. Light shone from the windows of the houses. There was the faintest sound of a piano playing.

The rain eased. I popped a peardrop into Harry's mouth and on we went.

I have a good memory – you will have noticed! – especially for those days. (As we get older, a brighter light, it seems, illuminates our childhood.) I can remember such details of our running away that it startles *me*. A small cat glowering at us from the bottom of a privet hedge. Harry spotting a penny on the pavement outside the chip shop and stooping to pick it up. Tiny hopping frogs on the towpath of the canal.

The canal, yes, I remember the canal. But the next bit is not so clear, not clear at all. It was a short cut, you see, between two bridges, one road and another. It was well-lit from the lights in a nearby factory car park. We went along the towpath (I remember) more slowly now. Harry had begun to flag, my leg was aching. The frogs hopped out. Some plopped into the water, I suppose. Harry maybe crouched to see them. But was I in front of him then or behind? Did I crouch too? Was it the slippery ground that did it or my weak leg sliding away beneath me? Or both? Or neither? Well, whatever it was it hardly matters now. What happened was, I fell into the canal.

Drowning

IT TAKES MORE TIME to drown than you would think. There's time, for instance, after your fight with the water is lost, to experience many things. To begin with, though, there's simply panic and shock. I may have slid into that canal like a canoe with barely a ripple, but there were ripples now and waves. I was thrashing and whirling about, desperate to regain the bank, and sinking.

The water was cold, foul-smelling, covered in scum. I disappeared beneath it. There was a pounding in my head, bright fractured light behind my eyes. I sank.

And rose again. I was coughing and spluttering. Slime and bits of weed were clinging to my hair and face. I sucked more air into my lungs and swallowed water. I sank again.

I was so weighted down, you see: my waterlogged clothes and shoes, my bag still over my shoulder, my heavy calipered leg, the stolen sixpences even.

The heaviness was winning. My struggles ceased. Time expanded.

I saw in quick and flickering succession, inside my flooded head, the image of Harry on the bank – poor Harry – poor, orphaned Harry (then there was *one*). And Dad, his mouth all comically puckered up, teaching me to whistle. And Dora, my tiny one-armed Bakelite doll. I saw Mrs Harris on a stepladder hanging paper chains. Leaping Rufus. A patch of sunlit sky. A little boat at sea. I saw my mother buttering bread. I saw Tom.

I saw Tom. I *did* see Tom. He was there in the water with me. And shouting (in the water, *under* it).

'Swim, Fran, swim!'

But Tom must know I couldn't swim,

even without this . . . heaviness.

'Fran!'

Tom's gravelly voice was a shock in my ear. My drifting foot grazed the bottom or, more likely, some submerged pram or other bit of rubbish. I tensed my leg, kicked and rose again. One final effort. My head broke the surface.

'Yell, Frances!' Tom shouted. 'Yell, yell, YELL!'

I rolled upon my back for a second and glimpsed the blue-black sky. And yelled.

The Hospital

I WAS RESCUED FROM the waters of the Tipton canal by thirty-seven-year-old Mr Arthur Finch, a self-employed carpenter of 109 Brass House Lane, West Bromwich. (I have confidence in these details. I still have the newspaper cutting.) Apparently Harry had raced back up onto the bridge seeking help. Meanwhile Mr Finch had come along the towpath on his bike, heard my cries and dived in fully clothed. His wife, Mrs Muriel Finch, was reported as being unsurprised by her husband's behaviour. He was always a hero in her eyes, she said.

One other thing, while I remember: Mr Finch, having got me onto the towpath, dived in again, convinced as he was that someone else was in there. He had heard *two* voices, you see.

I experienced nothing of the rescue itself, being unconscious even before my saviour reached me. (Those yells were literally my last gasp.) When I came round some hours later, I was in a hospital bed. The ward was dark, with pools and patches of light, green and yellow walls, two rows of beds along its length.

I lay quite still, staring up at the ceiling. After a time I noticed a huddled figure at the side of the bed. It was Marge, fast asleep with her glasses askew and her handbag in her lap. The bed felt cool, the sheets stretched taut like the sails of a ship, the pillow thin and hard. A baby was crying some-where. There was the sharp sour smell of disinfectant. I drifted off.

Dreaming. And in my dream I was drowning again, only this time in the sea. And Dad and Harry were looking for me, up and down the beach. And I was there. There! But they never saw me.

I woke again. Streaks of grey and pinkish light at the windows. Marge's seat was vacant. A nurse passed down the centre aisle carrying a tray. Tom was watching me from the end of the bed.

Tom, my other rescuer (no place for him, though, in the *Warley Weekly News*). He moved and stood beside me. Smiled, leant over, and put his hand on mine.

I felt it – did I? I did, though half asleep and woozy from the medicine they'd given me. It wasn't much of a touch, hardly 'substantial', more like the flimsiest, frailest piece of cloth falling on you; a feeling of graininess, texture. Not much, but something, surely, more than mere empty air.

The nurse came back and approached the bed. She stood where Tom was standing, took my pulse. Tom moved aside. He watched the nurse, waiting for her to leave. He gazed out of one of the rapidly brightening windows. He turned his collar down.

Getting Better

I WAS EXTREMELY ILL for a while, detained in the hospital for nearly three weeks. The swallowed water was responsible. I caught some kind of fever from it. That Tipton canal almost did for me twice over, you might say. But then I began to get well. Marge and Stan, and Harry too, came every evening to see me. Mrs Harris came with a basket of fruit. Later on she came again with a copy of *Black Beauty* that all the children in the school, she said, had clubbed together to buy. I seem to remember she brought two or three children with her. (I still have the book.)

Then what? Out of the hospital, back to home and school. Before I knew it, it was the summer holidays. Marge and Stan took us on a train to Weston-super-Mare. We stayed in a caravan. I'm not sure where they got the money from; Stan was still out of a job.

Speaking of money, those sixpences, the ones I took for running away with, were never mentioned. I've always wondered, did Marge most likely find them in my pocket, or had they disappeared into the canal? Are they there still, sunken treasure? Who knows.

Something else that was never mentioned was Canada. Odd letters still arrived but otherwise it just fell out of the conversation. I never knew why. Then in the autumn Stan got a job.

I guess we couldn't know it at the time, but all that business with the canal, the fever and so on was to prove the lowest point not just for me but for the others too. The curve of all our lives after that more or less went up.

So Stan got a job, and a good one, at Guest, Keen and Nettlefolds. A month or so later, with Christmas approaching, we moved into a new house, a council semi, with a garden all to itself backing onto the park. Spring came. Stan acquired a small greenhouse, Harry and I had our own little plots and Rufus took great delight in the prospect of the park, his absolutely favourite place for a walk.

In the summer it was Marge's turn for a new job. She gave up cleaning and went to work in a shop. Marge. I suspect I may have been too hard on Marge. Anyway, she improved. Her temper was still uncertain. She yelled at us at times but never hit us again. We became less afraid of her. Once she threw a teacup straight through the (closed) kitchen window for some reason or other – not at us, not at anybody. After which, appalled by her own action, she looked at me and both of us burst out laughing. (I could hardly ever remember Marge laughing before.)

As for Tom, he was his usual unusual self. He found his way to our new house, spent time with me and Harry in our now separate rooms, accompanied us to school. He disappeared too, sometimes for a whole week. On one occasion he found himself in the Plaza cinema in Brierley Hill watching a war movie. On another he spent the entire day at a cricket match, Warwickshire versus Surrey. Tom was not even interested in cricket.

*

Then, in the spring of 1958, surprising news: I'd passed the Eleven Plus (the entrance exam for the local grammar school). I was, it turned out, cleverer than we knew. Mrs Harris was flabbergasted. Rosalind likewise, although she also passed. Marge went mad . . . with delight. She it was who first read the letter and yelled to Stan about it and hurtled (yelling) up the stairs to me. Marge, I never thought to see the day, was proud of me.

That morning I went to school with a glow on my cheeks and my Eleven Plus letter in my hand. Tom walked beside me. It was then that for the very first time I noticed it: I was taller than him.

Tom's Compass

HE WAS TEN WHEN it happened, and I was nine and Harry was three. Now I was eleven and Harry was five and Tom was still ten. (Keep going: at the time of writing, I am fifty-two – good grief! – Harry is forty-six and Tom, wherever he is, is ten.)

That's how it was. That's what being a ghost, Tom discovered, was all about, or partly about. (He of course had noticed what was happening long before we did.)

So the years passed and we moved on and Tom stayed where he was, marooned. His appearance never changed, not one unruly hair on his head. His voice, though, modulated somewhat in time to a lighter, more normal pitch, either that or I just got used to it. His conversation became even quirkier, like random bits of a jigsaw puzzle or peculiar crossword clues. He would disappear now, often for weeks on end, and then show up looking dazed. He rarely spoke of his ghost life. Questions about it appeared unsettling to him. We gave up asking them.

I worried about him. He seemed so much smaller with the years, frailer, sadder. I wanted to help but never found the means. There again, how hard it is sometimes to capture the truth. For Tom was also funny and relaxed. It amused him to have this huge and hulking little sister, this giant of a baby brother. And he watched out for us still, charted his course to intersect our lives. He had no map perhaps, but he had a compass.

When I was thirteen, I had my caliper removed and replaced by a special shoe (a thicker sole and heel). Marge became manageress of the shop she worked in. At fourteen I started going out with

Roger Horsfield, my first boyfriend. Harry, now nine and soon to be the tallest of us all, was playing football every evening in the park. He was a prodigy already and later was to play for West Bromwich Albion reserves.

Rufus was by this time an elderly dog. He stumbled around, not seeing very well. The furniture was safe with him.

When I was fifteen, Rufus died.

Leaving

S O HERE I SIT forty years on writing all this down. It's late afternoon, October, a sudden sharpness in the air, red-golden leaves out on the lawn, my dear cat, Muggs, prowling the shrubbery.

And I begin to wonder, did these things happen? Did I see them, hear them, smell them? Have I *remembered* it, all of it, truly, as it really was? Is nothing made up?

I don't know. Harry, I mentioned earlier, has been reading what I've written and he confirms the gist of it. (But he was only three when it began.) Memories of course are insubstantial (like ghosts!). There again, things are real, and I still have my box. It's here beside me on the table as I write: the bracelet, the newspaper cutting, Tom's cigarette cards. And when I hold these items in my hand and spread them out . . . and smell them, I feel a rush of pure conviction. My doubts dissolve.

We buried Rufus in the garden, Harry and I. It was quite early in the morning. We agreed a spot with Stan and dug the hole. Rufus's little body was stiff already. (Rufus was a mongrel terrier, I don't believe I ever mentioned that.) He looked so normal, lying on his side, his stubby tail, the grey hair round his muzzle, his one brown-circled eye. We covered him over, patted the soil into place.

Rufus's ghost showed up in the garden on the following afternoon. I saw him from the kitchen window. There was only me in the house. I ran outside. It was midsummer, a hot and cloudless day. Rufus staggered towards me. I knelt and held out a hand. It was of course no use. Rufus blundered on and through me. His water bowl was still in its place outside the kitchen door. Poor Rufus reached the bowl, butted his head down into it and lapped vainly at the puddle of water it contained. After a while he gave up. Moments later, with a terrible slowed-down grinding sort of sound, Rufus barked.

For two days Rufus continued to appear before us (Harry and me), almost always in the garden. He was a pitiful sight: slow, stumbling, bewildered. He could not fathom his new relationship to people and things. He kept trying to make contact. On the evening of the third day, Tom arrived.

Rufus was lying on the little patch of slabs outside the kitchen door. Tom came up to him, knelt down and *ruffled his fur*. I saw the fur move. Rufus rolled over and almost managed a leap. He collided joyfully with Tom. I saw the impact. He licked Tom's hand. I saw the shine of his saliva on Tom's skin.

Tom took Rufus's lead out of his pocket; a ghostly lead for a ghostly dog. (Had it been there all those years?) Rufus quivered as he'd always done at the prospect of a walk. Tom gave me a smile and a wave. He led Rufus away, across the garden, through the fence and into the trees. A kite was dipping and swinging above them in the sky;

distant children shouting in the park.

We never saw Tom again (or Rufus), though we looked for him on and off for years. My brother's ghost is gone and it's all for the best. He's somewhere (that's the most you can say), has Rufus with him, and is working it out.

To

_____

From

_____

Real Questions...
Real Anwsers...

his
devotional

2

MINUTES A DAY
FOR TEENS

his devotional

2

MINUTES A DAY
FOR TEENS

Scripture quotations are taken from:

The Holy Bible, New King James Version (NKJV) Copyright © 1982 by Thomas Nelson, Inc. Used by permission.

Holy Bible, New Living Translation, (NLT) Copyright © 1996. Used by permission of Tyndale House Publishers, Inc., Wheaton, Illinois 60189. All rights reserved.

New Century Version®. (NCV) Copyright © 1987, 1988, 1991 by Word Publishing, a division of Thomas Nelson, Inc. All rights reserved. Used by permission.

The Message (MSG) This edition issued by contractual arrangement with NavPress, a division of The Navigators, U.S.A. Originally published by NavPress in English as THE MESSAGE: The Bible in Contemporary Language copyright 2002-2003 by Eugene Peterson. All rights reserved.

The Holman Christian Standard Bible™ (HCSB) Copyright © 1999, 2000, 2001 by Holman Bible Publishers. Used by permission.

Cover Design by Kim Russell / Wahoo Designs
Page Layout by Bart Dawson

ISBN 1-58334-193-5

Printed in the United States of America

Table of Contents

Introduction:

Two Minutes and Counting • 10

introduction:

2 Minutes and Counting

Okay, everybody knows you're a very busy guy. But here's a question: Can you squeeze two little minutes into your hectic schedule? If you're smart, the answer will be a resounding yes. Why? Because the two minutes in question are the minutes that you give to God!

God has a plan for everything, including you. And the more you talk to your Creator, the sooner He will help you figure out exactly what that plan is. So do yourself a favor: start talking. Now! As you begin that conversation, this little book can help.

This book contains 31 short devotional readings of particular interest to guys who, like you, are busy. Each chapter contains a Bible verse, a brief devotional reading, quotations from noted Christian men (plus quotes from a few women tossed in for good measure), and a prayer.

Do you have questions that you can't answer? Are you seeking to improve some aspect of your life? Do you want to be a better person *and* a better Christian? If so, ask for God's help and ask for it many times each day . . . starting with a regular, heartfelt morning devotional. Even two minutes is enough time to change your day . . . *and* your life.

INTRODUCTION

A Couple of Minutes for God

Be still, and know that I am God.
Psalm 46:10 NKJV

When it comes to spending time with God, are you a "squeezer" or a "pleaser"? Do you squeeze God into your schedule with a prayer before meals (and maybe, if you've got the time, with a quick visit to church on Sunday)? Or do you please God by talking to Him far more often than that? If you're wise, you'll form the habit of spending time with God every day. When you do, it will change your life.

This book asks that you give your undivided attention to God for *at least* two minutes each day. And make no mistake about it: The emphasis in the previous sentence should be placed on the words "at least." In truth, you should give God lots more time than a couple of minutes a day, but hey, it's a start!

Even if you're the busiest man on Planet Earth, you can still carve out a little time for God. And when you think about it, isn't that the very least you should do?

2 MINUTES A DAY

Think About It

Without solitude it is virtually impossible
to live a spiritual life. Solitude begins with
a time and a place for God, and him alone.
Henri Nouwen

Every morning I spend fifteen minutes
filling my mind full of God;
and so there's no room left for worry.
Howard Chandler Christy

When you meet with God, open the Bible.
Don't rely on your memory;
rely on those printed pages.
Charles Swindoll

A COUPLE OF MINUTES FOR GOD

And One More Thing . . .

Speed-reading may be a good thing,
but it was never meant for the Bible.
It takes calm, thoughtful, prayerful
meditation on the Word to extract
its deepest nourishment.

Vance Havner

A Prayer for Today

Lord, even when I'm very busy, I will slow
down and talk to You. I will let Your Word
be my guide. And as I spend time with you,
let me grow in faith and in wisdom, today
and every day. Amen

It's a Day
to Celebrate

Celebrate God all day, every day.
I mean, revel in him!

Philippians 4:4 msg

Do you feel like celebrating today? You should! Today and every day should be a day of prayer and praise as you consider the Good News of God's free gift: salvation through Jesus Christ.

Don't wait for birthdays or holidays— make every day a special day, including this one. Take time to pause and thank God for His gifts. And then demonstrate your gratitude by celebrating His creation, His blessings, and His love.

Think About It

All our life is a celebration for us;
we are convinced, in fact, that God
is always everywhere. We sing while
we work . . . we pray while we carry out
all life's other occupations.
St. Clement of Alexandria

Some of us seem so anxious about
avoiding hell that we forget to celebrate
our journey toward heaven.
Philip Yancey

I know nothing, except what everyone
knows—where God dances,
I should dance.
W. H. Auden

IT'S A DAY TO CELEBRATE

A Timely Tip

Share the Good News

While you're celebrating life, don't try and keep the celebration to yourself. Let other people know why you're rejoicing, and don't be bashful about telling them how *they* can rejoice, too.

A Prayer for Today

Dear Lord, You have given me lots of reasons to celebrate, and as a way of saying "Thank You," I *will* celebrate. I will be a joyful Christian, Lord, quick to smile and slow to frown. And, I will share my joy with my family, my friends, and my neighbors, this day and every day. Amen

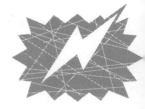

Why Am I Here?

You will show me the path of life;
in Your presence is fullness of joy;
at Your right hand are pleasures
forevermore.

Psalm 16:11 NKJV

"**What** does God want me to do with my life?" Maybe you've asked yourself this question . . . a lot. It's an easy question to ask but, for many of us, a tough question to answer. Why? Because God's plans aren't always clear to us. But even when we're wandering far from God's path, He has a plan to lead us back to Him.

Are you genuinely trying to figure out God's purpose for your life? If so, you can be sure that with God's help, you *will* eventually sort things out. So in the meantime, keep praying, and keep watching.

God's got big plans for you. Now, it's up to you and Him to work things out. And don't worry: the two of you, working together, can get the job done.

Think About It

It's incredible to realize that
what we do each day has meaning
in the big picture of God's plan.
Bill Hybels

We aren't just thrown on this earth
like dice tossed across a table.
We are lovingly placed here for a purpose.
Charles Swindoll

When God speaks to you through
the Bible, prayer, circumstances,
the church, or in some other way,
he has a purpose in mind for your life.
Henry Blackaby and Claude King

WHY AM I HERE?

Q: Why does my life sometimes seem like such a big mystery?

A: Because God isn't telling everything He knows. You can be sure that He's got a wonderful plan for you, but you can also be sure that He's keeping some things to Himself. Your job is to keep asking God for direction, and to take one step at a time in the direction that He leads. And remember this: If you're a believer, the ending to your story is *not* a mystery—it's a happy ending in heaven—so keep things in perspective.

A Prayer for Today

Lord, You've got something you want me to do—help me to figure out exactly what it is. Give me Your blessings and lead me along a path that is pleasing to You . . . today, tomorrow, and forever. Amen

Courage
for Today

Do not be afraid or discouraged.
For the LORD your God is
with you wherever you go.
Joshua 1:9 NLT

Being a godly guy in this difficult world is no easy task. Ours is a time of uncertainty and danger, a time when even the most courageous fellows have legitimate cause for concern. But as believers we can live courageously, knowing that we have been saved by a loving Father and His only begotten Son.

Are you troubled? Take your troubles to Him. Does the world seem to be trembling beneath your feet? Are you worried? Take those worries to God. Seek protection from the One who cannot be moved. The same God who created the universe will protect you *if* you ask Him . . . so ask Him. And then live courageously, knowing that even in these troubled times, God is always as near as your next breath.

Think About It

Fill you mind with thoughts of God
rather than thoughts of fear.
Norman Vincent Peale

A man who is intimate with God
will never be intimidated by men.
Leonard Ravenhill

Courage is contagious.
Billy Graham

The fear of God is the death
of every other fear.
C. H. Spurgeon

COURAGE FOR TODAY

Q: If God is good, why does He allow bad things to happen?

A: Sometimes, people do dumb or evil things, in *those* cases, it's obvious why bad stuff happens. But other times, bad things happen, and nobody is to blame. Sometimes, things *just happen* and we simply cannot know why. The Bible promises that when we finally get to heaven, we will understand all the reasons behind God's plans. But until then, we must simply trust Him, knowing that in the end, He will make things right.

A Prayer for Today

Lord, give me courage, even when I don't understand why things turn out like they do. No matter what happens, I still know Who's in charge: You. And until that day when I understand everything, I will live courageously, and trust You. Amen

The Right Kind of Example

You are the light that gives light to the world. In the same way, you should be a light for other people. Live so that they will see the good things you do and will praise your Father in heaven.

Matthew 5:14, 16 NCV

Okay, here's a question: What kind of example are you? Are you the kind of guy whose life serves as a powerful example of decency and morality? Are you a guy whose behavior serves as a positive role model for others? Are you the kind of guy whose actions, day in and day out, are based upon integrity, fidelity, and a love for the Lord? If so, you are not only blessed by God, but you are also a powerful force for good in a world that desperately needs positive influences such as yours.

Phillips Brooks advised, "Be such a man, and live such a life, that if every man were such as you, and every life a life like yours, this earth would be God's Paradise." And that's sound advice because our families and friends are watching . . . and so, for that matter, is God.

Think About It

More depends on my walk than my talk.
D. L. Moody

We urgently need people who encourage
and inspire us to move toward God
and away from the world's
enticing pleasures.
Jim Cymbala

There is too much sermonizing and
too little witnessing. People do not come
to Christ at the end of an argument.
Vance Havner

THE RIGHT KIND OF EXAMPLE

A Timely Tip

Think ahead:

Before you do something, ask yourself this question: "Will I be ashamed if everybody, including my family, finds out?" If the answer to that question is "Yes," don't do it!

A Prayer for Today

Lord, make me a worthy example to my family and friends. And, let my words and my actions show people how my life has been changed by You. I will praise You, Father, by following in the footsteps of Your Son. Let others see Him through me. Amen

Temper Tantrums

Foolish people lose their tempers,
but wise people control theirs.
Proverbs 29:11 NCV

his devotional

Temper tantrums are usually unproductive, unattractive, unforgettable, and unnecessary. Perhaps that's why Proverbs 16:32 states that, "Controlling your temper is better than capturing a city" (NCV).

If you've allowed anger to become a regular visitor at your house, today you must pray for wisdom, for patience, and for a heart that is so filled with love and forgiveness that it contains no room for bitterness. God will help you terminate your tantrums if you ask Him to. And God can help you perfect your ability to be patient if you ask Him to. So ask Him, and then wait patiently for the ever-more-patient you to arrive.

Think About It

Why lose your temper if, by doing so,
you offend God, annoy other people,
give yourself a bad time . . .
and, in the end, have to find it again?
Josemaria Escriva

Anger is the noise of the soul;
the unseen irritant of the heart;
the relentless invader of silence.
Max Lucado

No one heals himself by
wounding another.
St. Ambrose

Bitterness and anger, usually over
trivial things, make havoc of homes,
churches, and friendships.
Warren Wiersbe

TEMPER TANTRUMS

Count to ten . . . but don't stop there: If you're angry with someone, don't say the first thing that comes to your mind. Instead, catch your breath and start counting until you are once again in control of your temper. If you count to a thousand and you're still counting, go to bed! You'll feel better in the morning.

A Prayer for Today

Lord, I can be so impatient, and I can become so angry. Calm me down, Lord, and give me the maturity and the wisdom to be a patient, forgiving Christian. Just as You have forgiven me, Father, let me forgive others so that I can follow the example of Your Son. Amen

The Rule That's Golden

Here is a simple rule-of-thumb for behavior: Ask yourself what you want people to do for you, then grab the initiative and do it for them. Add up God's Law and Prophets and this is what you get.

Matthew 7:12 MSG

his devotional

Is the Golden Rule your rule, or is it just another Bible verse that goes in one ear and out the other? Jesus made Himself perfectly clear: He instructed you to treat other people in the same way that you want to be treated. But sometimes, especially when you're feeling pressure from friends, or when you're tired or upset, obeying the Golden Rule can seem like an impossible task—but it's not.

God wants each of us to treat other people with respect, kindness, and courtesy. He wants us to rise above our own imperfections, and He wants us to treat others with unselfishness and love. To make it short and sweet, God wants us to obey the Golden Rule, and He knows we can do it.

So if you're wondering how to treat someone else, ask the person you see every time you look into the mirror. The answer you receive will tell you exactly what to do.

2 MINUTES A DAY

Think About It

It is wrong for anyone to be anxious
to receive more from his neighbor
than he himself is willing to give to God.
St. Francis of Assisi

Anything done for another is done
for oneself.
Pope John Paul II

Make the most of today.
Translate your good intentions
into actual good deeds.
Grenville Kleiser

THE RULE THAT'S GOLDEN

And One More Thing . . .

Do all the good you can.
By all the means you can.
In all the ways you can.
In all the places you can.
At all the times you can.
To all the people you can.
As long as ever you can.
John Wesley

A Prayer for Today

Lord, in all aspects of my life, let me treat others as I wish to be treated. The Golden Rule is Your rule, Father; let me make it mine. Amen

Where Is God?

Fear not, for I am with you;
Be not dismayed, for I am your God.
I will strengthen you.
Isaiah 41:10 NKJV

Do you ever wonder if God is really here? If so, you're not the first person to think such thoughts. In fact, some of the biggest heroes in the Bible had their doubts—and so, perhaps, will you. But when questions arise and doubts begin to creep into your mind, remember this: God hasn't gone on vacation; He hasn't left town; and He doesn't have an unlisted number. You can talk with Him any time you feel like it. In fact, He's right here, right now, listening to your thoughts and prayers, watching over your every move.

Sometimes, you will allow yourself to become *very* busy, and that's when you may be tempted to ignore God. But, when you quiet yourself long enough to acknowledge His presence, God will touch your heart and restore your spirits. By the way, He's ready to talk right now. Are you?

Think About It

Our battles are first won or lost in the secret
places of our will in God's presence,
never in full view of the world.
Oswald Chambers

When we are in the presence of God,
removed from distractions, we are able
to hear him more clearly, and a secure
environment has been established for
the young and broken places
in our hearts to surface.
John Eldredge

God's presence is with you, but
you have to make a choice to believe—
and I mean, really believe—that this is true.
This conscious decision is your alone.
Bill Hybels

WHERE IS GOD?

Q: If God is everywhere, why does He sometimes seem so far away?

A: The answer to that question, of course, has nothing to do with God and everything to do with us. God sometimes seems far away because we have allowed ourselves to become distant from Him, not vice versa.

A Prayer for Today

Dear Lord, You are with me when I am strong and when I am weak. You never leave my side, even when it seems to me that You are far away. Today and every day, let me trust Your promises and let me feel Your love. Amen

A Prayer for Perseverance

Even though good people may
be bothered by trouble seven times,
they are never defeated.
Proverbs 24:16 NCV

A well-lived life is like a marathon, not a sprint—it calls for preparation, determination, and, of course, *lots* of perseverance. As an example of perfect perseverance, we Christians need look no further than our Savior, Jesus Christ.

Jesus finished what He began. Despite His suffering, despite the shame of the cross, Jesus was steadfast in His faithfulness to God. We, too, must remain faithful, especially during times of hardship. Sometimes, God may answer our prayers with silence, and when He does, we must patiently persevere.

Are you facing a tough situation? If so, remember this: whatever your problem, God can handle it. Your job is to keep persevering until He does.

Think About It

In the Bible, patience is not a passive
acceptance of circumstances.
It is a courageous perseverance
in the face of suffering and difficulty.
Warren Wiersbe

All rising to a great place is
by a winding stair.
Francis Bacon

Battles are won in the trenches,
in the grit and grime of courageous
determination; they are won
day by day in the arena of life.
Charles Swindoll

By perseverance, the snail reached the ark.
C. H. Spurgeon

A PRAYER FOR PERSEVERANCE

Q: If I can't see a solution to a particular problem, why shouldn't I go ahead and give up now?

A: Because things change, and that includes your problems. Even if you can't see a perfect solution today, you may stumble over a perfect solution tomorrow, so don't give up at the first sign of trouble.

A Prayer for Today

Lord, some days I feel like there's no way I can win. But when I'm discouraged, let me turn to You for strength, courage, and faith. When I find my strength in You, Lord, I am protected, today and forever. Amen

When Guys (or Girls) Are Cruel

Stop judging others, and you will not
be judged. Stop criticizing others,
or it will all come back on you.
If you forgive others, you will be forgiven.

Luke 6:37 NLT

F a c e it: Sometimes people can be cruel . . . *very* cruel. When other people are unkind to you *or* to your friends, you may be tempted to strike back, either verbally *or* physically. Don't do it! Instead, remember that God corrects other people's behaviors in His own way, and He doesn't need your help (even if you're totally convinced you're "in the right"). Remember that God has commanded you to forgive others, just as you, too, must sometimes seek forgiveness from others.

So, when other people behave cruelly, foolishly, or impulsively—as they will from time to time—don't start swinging *or* screaming. Speak up for yourself as politely as you can, and walk away. Next, forgive everybody as quickly as you can. Then, get on with your life, and leave the rest up to God.

Think About It

Turn your attention upon yourself
and beware of judging the deeds of
other men, for in judging others a man
labors vainly, often makes mistakes,
and easily sins; whereas, in judging
and taking stock of himself he does
something that is always profitable.
Thomas à Kempis

You have no idea how big
the other fellow's troubles are.
B. C. Forbes

When a man points a finger at
someone else, he should remember
that four of his fingers
are pointing at himself.
Louis Nizer

WHEN GUYS (OR GIRLS) ARE CRUEL

And One More Thing . . .

To hold on to hate and resentments is
to throw a monkey wrench
into the machinery of life.

E. Stanley Jones

A Prayer for Today

Lord, just as You have forgiven me,
I am going to forgive others. When
I forgive others, I not only obey Your
commandments, but I also free myself from
bitterness and regret. Forgiveness is Your
way, Lord, and I will make it my way, too.
Amen

Overcoming the Fear of Failure

For God has not given us a spirit of fear,
but of power and of love and
of a sound mind.

2 Timothy 1:7 NLT

His adoring fans called him the "Sultan of Swat." He was Babe Ruth, the baseball player who set records for home runs *and* strikeouts. Babe's philosophy was simple. He said, "Never let the fear of striking out get in your way." That's smart advice on the diamond *or* off.

It's never wise to take *foolish* risks (so buckle up, slow down, and don't do anything stupid!). But when it comes to the game of life, you should not let the fear of failure keep you from taking your swings.

Today, ask God for the courage to step beyond the boundaries of your self-doubts. Ask Him to guide you to a place where you can realize your full potential—a place where you are freed from the fear of failure. Ask Him to do His part, and promise Him that you will do your part. Don't ask Him to lead you to a "safe" place; ask Him to lead you to the "right" place . . . and remember: those two places are seldom the same.

2 MINUTES A DAY

Think About It

God is a specialist; He is well able to work our failures into His plans. Often the doorway to success is entered through the hallway of failure.

Erwin Lutzer

Never imagine that you can be a loser by trusting in God.

C. H. Spurgeon

Do not be one of those who, rather than risk failure, never attempt anything.

Thomas Merton

No matter how badly we have failed, we can always get up and begin again. Our God is the God of new beginnings.

Warren Wiersbe

OVERCOMING THE FEAR OF FAILURE

Q: When I mess up, why am I so afraid of what my friends will think?

A: Maybe it's because you're *too concerned* about what people think and *not concerned enough* about what God thinks. Instead of worrying about what "they" think (whoever "they" are), worry more about what "He" thinks (He, of course, being God). After all, whom should you *really* be trying to impress—"them" or Him?

A Prayer for Today

Dear Lord, even when I'm afraid of failure, give me the courage to try. Remind me that with You by my side, I really have nothing to fear. So today, Father, I will live courageously as I place my faith in You. Amen

Family Matters

> You must choose for yourselves
> today whom you will serve . . .
> as for me and my family,
> we will serve the Lord.
>
> **Joshua 24:15 NCV**

Okay admit it: Sometimes family life can be a little frustrating. Even when everybody's trying to do their best, no family is perfect, not even yours. But remember this: Despite the occasional frustrations, disappointments, and hurt feelings of family life, your clan is God's gift to you. That little band of men, women, kids, and babies is a priceless treasure on temporary loan from the Father above. Give thanks to the Giver for the gift of family . . . and act accordingly.

Think About It

Apart from religious influence,
the family is the most important
influence on society.
Billy Graham

You don't choose your family.
They are God's gift to you,
as you are to them.
Desmond Tutu

The mind of Christ is to be learned
in the family. Strength of character
may be acquired at work, but
beauty of character is learned at home.
Henry Drummond

FAMILY MATTERS

Q: What if I'm having *really* big problems with my family?

A: You've simply *got* to keep talking things over, even if it's hard. And, remember: what seems like a mountain today may turn out to be a molehill tomorrow.

A Prayer for Today

Lord, You have given me a family that cares for me and loves me. Thank You, Father. Let me love all the members of my family *despite their imperfections*, and let them love me *despite mine*. Amen

Faith for the Future

"I say this because I know what
I am planning for you," says the Lord.
"I have good plans for you, not plans
to hurt you. I will give you hope
and a good future."
Jeremiah 29:11 NCV

How bright is your future? Well, if you're a faithful believer, God's plans for you are so bright that you'd better wear shades. But here's an important question: How bright do *you* believe your future to be? Are you expecting a terrific tomorrow, or are you dreading a terrible one? The answer you give will have a powerful impact on the way tomorrow turns out.

Do you trust in the ultimate goodness of God's plan for your life? Will you face tomorrow's challenges with optimism and hope? You should. After all, God created you for a very important reason: *His* reason. And you still have important work to do: *His* work.

Today, as you live in the present and look to the future, remember that God has an amazing plan for you. Act—and believe—accordingly.

2 MINUTES A DAY

Think About It

The Christian believes in a fabulous future.
Billy Graham

The strength and happiness of a man
consists in finding out the way in which
God is going, and going that way too.
Henry Ward Beecher

Every day should be a fantastic adventure
for us because we're in the middle of
God's unfolding plan for the ages.
John MacArthur

FAITH FOR THE FUTURE

And One More Thing . . .

Wherever you are, be all there.
Live to the hilt every situation
you believe to be the will of God.
Jim Elliot

A Prayer for Today

Lord, sometimes when I think about the future, I worry. Today, I will do a better job of trusting You. If I become discouraged, I will turn to You. If I am afraid, I will seek strength in You. You are my Father, and I will place my hope, my trust, and my faith in You. Amen

Grace for Today . . . and Forever

For by grace you have been saved
through faith, and that not of yourselves;
it is the gift of God.

Ephesians 2:8 NKJV

God's grace is not earned; it's a gift—and thank goodness for that! To earn God's gift of eternal life would be far beyond the abilities of even the most righteous guy or girl. Thankfully, God's grace is not an earthly reward for good behavior; it is a spiritual gift that can be accepted by believers who dedicate themselves to God through Christ. When we accept Christ into our hearts, we are saved by His grace.

As you think about the day ahead, praise God for His blessings. He is the Giver of all things good. Praise Him today and forever.

Think About It

Our transformation of heart is utterly
and completely a work of grace.
Richard Foster

They travel lightly whom
God's grace carries.
Thomas à Kempis

You will never be called upon to
give anyone more grace
than God has already given you.
Max Lucado

GRACE FOR TODAY . . . AND FOREVER

And One More Thing . . .

All men who live with any degree
of serenity live by some assurance of grace.
Reinhold Niebuhr

A Prayer for Today

Lord, I'm only here on earth for a brief visit. Heaven is my real home. You've given me the gift of eternal life through Your Son Jesus. I accept Your gift, Lord. And I'll share Your Good News so that others, too, might come to know Christ's healing touch. Amen

Standing Up for My Beliefs

All those who stand before others
and say they believe in me,
I will say before my Father in heaven
that they belong to me.
Matthew 10:32 NCV

his devotional

Sometimes it's hard being a Christian, especially when the world keeps pumping out messages that are contrary to your faith.

The media is working around the clock in an attempt to rearrange your priorities. The media says that your appearance is all-important, that your clothes are all-important, that your car is all-important, and that partying is all-important. But guess what? Those messages are lies. The "all-important" things in your life have little to do with parties and appearances. The all-important things in life have to do with your faith, your family, and your future.

Are you willing to stand up for your faith? Are you willing to stand up and be counted, not just in church, where it's relatively easy to be a Christian, but also out there in the "real" world, where it's hard? Hopefully so, because you owe it to God *and* you owe it to yourself.

2 MINUTES A DAY

Think About It

First thing every morning before you arise,
say out loud, "I believe," three times.
Norman Vincent Peale

As the body lives by breathing,
so the soul lives by believing.
Thomas Brooks

One man with beliefs is equal
to a thousand with only interests.
John Stuart Mill

STANDING UP FOR MY BELIEFS

A Timely Tip

Put Peer Pressure to Work For You:

Make up your mind to hang out with people who will put pressure on you to become a better person.

A Prayer for Today

Dear Lord, today I will worry *less* about pleasing other people and *more* about pleasing you. I will stand up for my beliefs, and I will honor You with my thoughts, my actions, and my prayers. And I will worship You, Father, with thanksgiving in my heart, this day and forever. Amen

16

In a Hurry to Learn Patience

It is better to be patient than powerful;
it is better to have self-control
than to conquer a city.

Proverbs 16:32 NLT

Are you a perfectly patient fellow? If so, feel free to skip the rest of this page. But if you're not, here's something to think about: If you *really* want to become a more patient person, God is ready and willing to help.

God is always ready to help you become a better person. In fact, the Bible promises that when you sincerely seek God's help, He will give you the things you need. So, if you want to become a more patient (and mature) person, bow your head and start praying about it. Then rest assured that with God's help, you can change for the better . . . and that you will!

Think About It

Our patience will achieve more
than our force.
Edmund Burke

The next time you're disappointed,
don't panic and don't give up.
Just be patient and let God remind you
he's still in control.
Max Lucado

Teach us, O Lord, the disciplines
of patience, for to wait is often harder
than to work.
Peter Marshall

IN A HURRY TO LEARN PATIENCE

A Timely Tip

Take a deep breath, a very deep breath:

If you think you're about to say or do something you'll regret later, slow down and take a deep breath, or two deep breaths, or ten, or . . . well you get the idea.

A Prayer for Today

Slow me down, Lord, so that I might feel your presence and Your peace. When I am hurried, angered, or discouraged, keep me mindful of Your blessings, Your commandments, Your mercy, and Your Son. Amen

When I Fall Short

For all have sinned
and fall short of the glory of God.

Romans 3:23 HCSB

his devotional

Sometimes, even if you're a very good guy, you're going to mess up. And when you do, God is always ready to forgive you—He'll do His part, but you should be willing to do your part, too. Here's what you need to do.

1. If you have been engaging in sinful behavior, cease and desist—STOP!

2. If you made a mistake, learn from it and don't repeat it (that's called getting smarter).

3. If you've hurt somebody, apologize and ask for forgiveness (that's called doing the right thing).

4. Ask for God's forgiveness, too (He'll give it whenever you ask, but you must ask).

Have you messed something up? If so, today is the perfect day to make things right with everybody (and the word "everybody" includes yourself, your family, your friends, and your God).

2 MINUTES A DAY

Think About It

An exalted view of God brings a clear view of sin and a realistic view of self.
Henry Blackaby

Never has the world seen another tyrant comparable to sin.
C. H. Spurgeon

A recovery of the old sense of sin is essential to Christianity.
C. S. Lewis

The simple fact is that if we sow a lifestyle that is in direct disobedience to God's revealed Word, we ultimately reap disaster.
Charles Swindoll

WHEN I FALL SHORT

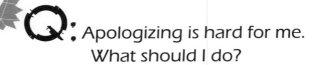

Q: Apologizing is hard for me. What should I do?

A: Even if you're not sure exactly what to say, and even if it's hard, apologize sooner rather than later—then, everybody can get on with their lives, including you.

A Prayer for Today

Dear Lord, I am not perfect. When I have sinned, let me repent my mistakes, and let me seek forgiveness—first from You, then from others, and finally from myself. Amen

Why God Gave Us Gifts

Do not neglect the gift that is in you.
1 Timothy 4:14 NKJV

F a c e it: You've got an array of talents that need to be refined. All people possess special gifts—bestowed from the Father above—and you are no exception. But, your gift is no guarantee of success; it must be cultivated—by you—or it will go unused . . . and God's gift to you will be squandered.

Today, make a promise to yourself that you will earnestly seek to discover the talents that God has given you. Then, nourish those talents and make them grow. Finally, vow to share your gifts with the world for as long as God gives you the power to do so. After all, the best way to say "Thank You" for God's gifts is to use them.

Think About It

We must not only give what we have,
we must also give what we are.
Désiré Joseph Mercier

God is still in the process of dispensing gifts,
and He uses ordinary individuals like us to
develop those gifts in other people.
Howard Hendricks

Somehow we human beings are never
happier than when we are expressing
the deepest gifts that are truly us.
Os Guinness

When God crowns our merits,
he is crowning nothing other than his gifts.
St. Augustine

WHY GOD GAVE US GIFTS

A Timely Tip

Converting Talent Into Skill Requires Work:

Remember this: "What we are is God's gift to us; what we become is our gift to God." You should work diligently to ensure that your gifts to God are worthy of the Giver.

A Prayer for Today

Lord, you have given me gifts—let me discover them and use them. Your gifts are priceless and eternal. I will do my best to use them to the glory of Your kingdom, today and forever. Amen

When Times Are Tough

Jesus said, "Don't let your hearts be troubled. Trust in God, and trust in me."

John 14:1 NCV

Are you a guy who has faced some tough times? If so, welcome to the club! From time to time, everybody faces adversity, discouragement, or disappointment. And that's where God comes in.

God loves you, and in times of hardship, He will protect you. When you are troubled, or weak, or sorrowful, God is always with you. Open your heart to Him, and build your life on the rock that cannot be shaken . . . trust in God. Always.

Think About It

If you learn to trust God with
a child-like dependence on Him as
your loving heavenly Father,
no trouble can destroy you.
Billy Graham

The more wisdom enters our hearts,
the more we will be able to trust
our hearts in difficult situations.
John Eldredge

When you accept disappointment,
when you trust God, and when you yield
to Him, you leave something behind
to help others in the battles of life.
Warren Wiersbe

WHEN TIMES ARE TOUGH

And One More Thing . . .

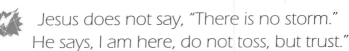

Jesus does not say, "There is no storm."
He says, I am here, do not toss, but trust."
Vance Havner

A Prayer for Today

Lord, sometimes life is tough . . . *very* tough. But even when I can't see any hope for the future, You are always with me. And, I can live courageously because I know that there is nothing that will happen to me today that You and I, working together, can't handle. Amen

20

Strength
for Today

I am able to do all things through
Him who strengthens me.

Philippians 4:13 HCSB

Where do you go to find strength? The gym? The health food store? The expresso bar? There's a better source of strength, of course, and that source is God. He is a never-ending source of strength and courage *if* you call upon Him.

Have you "tapped in" to the power of God? Have you turned your life and your heart over to Him, or are you muddling along under your own power? The answer to this question will determine the quality of your life here on earth *and* the destiny of your life throughout all eternity. So start tapping in—and remember that when it comes to strength, God is the Ultimate Source.

Think About It

Our Lord never drew power from Himself,
He drew it always from His Father.
Oswald Chambers

Jesus is all the world to me, my life, my joy,
my all; He is my strength from day to day,
without Him I would fall.
Will L. Thompson

God is great and God is powerful,
but we must invite him to be powerful
in our lives. His strength is always there,
but it's up to us to provide a channel
through which that power can flow.
Bill Hybels

STRENGTH FOR TODAY

A Timely Tip

Getting enough sleep?

If your fuse is chronically short, of if you're always tired, perhaps you need a little more shuteye. Try this experiment: Turn off the television and go to bed at a reasonable hour. You'll be amazed at how good you feel when you get eight hours of sleep.

A Prayer for Today

Lord, sometimes life is difficult. Sometimes, I am worried, weak, or heartbroken. But, when I lift my eyes to You, Father, You strengthen me and lift me up. Today, I turn to You, Lord, for strength, for hope, and for the promise of salvation. Amen

21

Forgive
and Forget?

Be kind and loving to each other,
and forgive each other just as
God forgave you in Christ.
Ephesians 4:32 NCV

Have you heard the saying, "Forgive and forget"? Well, it's certainly easier said than done. It's easy to talk about forgiving somebody, but actually forgiving that person can be much harder to do. And when it comes to forgetting, forget about it!

Sometimes, it's impossible to forget the things that other people have done to hurt us. But even if we *can't* forget, we *can* forgive. And that's exactly what God teaches us to do.

Think About It

Forget the faults of others by
remembering your own.
John Bunyan

God forgets the past. Imitate him.
Max Lucado

Not the power to remember, but
its very opposite, the power to forget,
is a necessary condition for our existence.
St. Basil

Learning how to forgive and forget is
one of the secrets of a happy Christian life.
Warren Wiersbe

FORGIVE AND FORGET?

Q: What if it's *really* hard to forgive somebody?

A: If forgiveness were easy, everybody would be doing it—but it's not always easy to forgive and forget. If you simply can't seem to forgive somebody, pray about it . . . and keep praying about it . . . until God helps you do the right thing.

A Prayer for Today

Lord, when I have trouble forgiving someone, when I'm discouraged, or tired, or angry, let me turn to You for strength, for patience, for wisdom, and for love. Amen

22

Stuff, Stuff, and More Stuff

The thing you should want most is
God's kingdom and doing what
God wants. Then all these other things
you need will be given to you.

Matthew 6:33 NCV

How much stuff is too much stuff? Well, if your desire for stuff is getting in the way of your desire to know God, then you've got too much stuff—it's as simple as that.

Do you find yourself wrapped up in the concerns of the material world? If so, it's time to reorder your priorities by turning your thoughts and your prayers to more important matters. And, it's time to begin storing up riches that will endure throughout eternity: the spiritual kind.

Think About It

The characteristic of the life of a saint
is essentially elemental simplicity.
Oswald Chambers

Don't be anxious about what you have,
but about what you are.
Pope Gregory the Great

Theirs is an endless road, a hopeless maze,
who seek for goods before
they seek for God.
St. Bernard of Clairvaux

It is better to be a poor man
and a rich Christian than a rich man
and a poor Christian.
Thomas Brooks

STUFF, STUFF, AND MORE STUFF

A Timely Tip

Stuff 101:

The world says, "Buy more stuff." God says, "Stuff isn't important." Believe God.

A Prayer for Today

Lord, my greatest possession is my relationship with You through Jesus Christ. You have promised that when I seek Your kingdom and Your righteousness, You will give me the things that I need. I will trust You completely, Lord, for my needs, both material and spiritual, this day and always. Amen

Time to Think . . . and to Pray

Be cheerful no matter what;
pray all the time; thank God no matter
what happens. This is the way God
wants you who belong to
Christ Jesus to live.

1 Thessalonians 5:16-18 MSG

How do you start your day? Do you sleep till the last possible moment, then leap out of the bed, throw on some clothes, and hit the road? If so, you're missing out on one of life's great pleasures: spending time each morning with God.

Each new day is a gift from God, and if you're wise, you'll spend a few quiet moments thanking the Giver. It's a wonderful way to start your day *and* to prioritize your life.

Think About It

If we really believe not only that God exists but also that God is actively present in our lives—healing, teaching, and guiding—we need to set aside a time and space to give God our undivided attention.
Henri Nouwen

Some of the best times in prayer are wordless times.
Charles Swindoll

Half an hour of listening to God is essential except when one is very busy. Then, a full hour is needed.
St. Francis of Sales

TIME TO THINK . . . AND TO PRAY

Q: Have you been too busy for a daily meeting with God?

A: If so, it's time to reorder your priorities. Make a promise to yourself that you will begin each day with a morning devotional. A regular time of quiet reflection and prayer will allow you to praise your Creator, to focus your thoughts, and to seek God's guidance on matters great and small.

A Prayer for Today

Dear Lord, every day of my life is a journey with You. I will take time today to think, to pray, and to study Your Word. Guide my steps, Father, and keep me mindful that today offers yet another opportunity to celebrate Your blessings, Your love, and Your Son. Amen

The Perfect Perfectionist

Those who wait for perfect weather will never plant seeds; those who look at every cloud will never harvest crops. Plant early in the morning, and work until evening, because you don't know if this or that will succeed. They might both do well.

Ecclesiastes 11:4, 6 NCV

his devotional

The difference between perfection-ism and excellence is the difference between a life of frustration and a life of satisfaction. Only one earthly being ever lived life to perfection, and He was the Son of God. The rest of us have fallen short of God's standard and need to be accepting of our own limitations as well as the limitations of others. God is perfect; we human beings are not. May we live—and forgive—accordingly.

Think About It

The happiest people in the world are not those who have no problems, but the people who have learned to live with those things that are less than perfect.
James Dobson

We shall never come to the perfect man til we come to the perfect world.
Matthew Henry

What makes a Christian a Christian is not perfection but forgiveness.
Max Lucado

A good garden may have some weeds.
Thomas Fuller

THE PERFECT PERFECTIONIST

Lighten Up!

The world isn't perfect; your family and friends aren't perfect; and you aren't perfect—and that's okay: We'll all have plenty of time to be perfect in heaven. Until them, we should all be compassionate, forgiving Christians.

A Prayer for Today

Lord, this world has so many expectations of me, but today I will not seek to meet the world's expectations; I will do my best to meet Your expectations. I will make You my ultimate priority, Lord, by serving You, by praising You, by loving You, and by obeying You. Amen

Slow Down and Think

People with good sense restrain
their anger.

Proverbs 19:11 NLT

Are you, at times, just a little bit impulsive? Do you sometimes leap before you look? If so, God wants to have a little chat with you.

God's Word is clear: As believers, we are called to lead lives of discipline, diligence, moderation, and maturity. But the world often tempts us to behave otherwise. Everywhere we turn, or so it seems, we are faced with powerful temptations to behave in undisciplined, ungodly ways.

God's Word instructs us to be disciplined in our thoughts and our actions; God's Word warns us against the dangers of impulsive behavior. As believers in a just God, we should act—*and react*—accordingly.

Think About It

By a tranquil mind, I mean nothing else
than a mind well ordered.
Marcus Aurelius

We will always experience regret when
we live for the moment and
do not weigh our words and deeds
before we give them life.
Lisa Bevere

You have to allow a certain amount of time
in which you are doing nothing in order
to have things occur to you,
to let your mind think.
Mortimer Adler

SLOW DOWN AND THINK

A Timely Tip

Put the brakes on impulsive behavior . . .

Before impulsive behavior puts the brakes on you.

A Prayer for Today

Lord, sometimes I can be an impulsive person. Slow me down, calm me down, and help me make wise decisions . . . today and every day of my life. Amen

Service
With
a Smile

The greatest among you will be
your servant. Whoever exalts himself
will be humbled, and whoever humbles
himself will be exalted.

Matthew 23:11-12 HCSB

Are you excited about serving God? You should be. As a believer living in today's challenging world, you have countless opportunities to honor your Father in Heaven by serving Him.

Far too many Christians seem bored with their faith and stressed by their service. Don't allow yourself to become one of them! Serve God with thanksgiving in your heart and a smile on your lips. Make your service to Him a time of celebration and thanksgiving. Worship your Creator by working for Him, joyfully, faithfully, and often.

Think About It

If the attitude of servanthood is learned,
by attending to God as Lord,
then, serving others will develop
as a very natural way of life.
Eugene Peterson

There are times when we are called
to love, expecting nothing in return.
There are times when we are called
to give money to people who will never
say thanks, to forgive those who won't
forgive us, to come early and stay late
when no one else notices.
Max Lucado

SERVICE WITH A SMILE

A Timely Tip

You can't just talk about it:

In order to be an effective servant, you must start serving . . . *now* . . . and that means today, not tomorrow.

A Prayer for Today

Lord, when Jesus humbled Himself and became a servant, He also became an example for me. Let me be a humble servant to my loved ones, to my friends, and to those in need. Amen

2 MINUTES A DAY

A World Filled With Temptations

But remember that the temptations that come into your life are no different from what others experience. And God is faithful. He will keep the temptation from becoming so strong that you can't stand up against it. When you are tempted, he will show you a way out so that you will not give in to it.

1 Corinthians 10:13 NLT

his devotional

Is it very hard to bump into temptation in this wacky world of ours? Nope, it's not very hard at all. The devil and his helpers are working overtime these days while causing pain and heartache in more places and in more ways than ever before. As Christians, we must remain strong.

Not only must we resist Satan when he confronts us, but we must also avoid those places where Satan can most easily tempt us. As believing Christians, we must beware, and we must earnestly wrap ourselves in the protection of God's Holy Word. When we do, we are secure.

Think About It

He does not keep us from temptation,
but He can keep us in temptation.
Vance Havner

Guard your eyes, since they are
the windows through which sin enters
into the soul. Never look curiously on those
things which are contrary to modesty,
even slightly.
St. John Bosco

But suppose we do sin. Suppose we slip
and fall. Suppose we yield to temptation
for a moment. What happens?
We have to confess that sin.
Billy Graham

A WORLD FILLED WITH TEMPTATIONS

A Timely Tip

We Live in a "Temptation Nation"

At every turn in the road, or so it seems, somebody is trying to tempt you with something. Your job is to steer clear of temptation . . . and to *keep steering clear* as long as you live.

A Prayer for Today

Lord, temptation is everywhere! Help me turn from it and to run from it! Let me keep Christ in my heart, and let me put the devil in his place: far away from me! Amen

2 MINUTES A DAY

Spiritual Maturity

Grow in grace and understanding
of our Master and Savior, Jesus Christ.
Glory to the Master, now and forever! Yes!

2 Peter 3:18 MSG

his devotional

When it comes to your faith, God doesn't intend for you to stand still. He wants you to keep moving and growing. In fact, God's plan for you includes a lifetime of prayer, praise, and spiritual growth.

As a Christian, you should continue to grow in the love and the knowledge of your Savior as long as you live. How? By studying God's Word every day, by obeying His commandments, and by allowing His Son to reign over your heart, that's how.

Are you continually seeking to become a more mature believer? Hopefully so, because that's exactly what you owe to yourself *and* to God . . . but not necessarily in that order.

2 MINUTES A DAY

Think About It

Spiritual growth consists most in
the growth of the root,
which is out of sight.
Matthew Henry

God loves us the way we are,
but He loves us too much
to leave us that way.
Leighton Ford

Spiritual growth is the process
of replacing lies with truth.
Rick Warren

SPIRITUAL MATURITY

And One More Thing . . .

Ask the God who made you
to keep remaking you.
Norman Vincent Peale

A Prayer for Today

Lord, help me to keep growing spiritually and emotionally. Let me live according to Your Word, and let me grow in my faith every day that I live. Amen

Thanksgiving Day by Day

It is good to give thanks to the LORD,
to sing praises to the Most High.

Psalm 92:1 NLT

his devotional

Are you basically a thankful guy? Do you appreciate the stuff you've got and the life that you're privileged to live? You should. After all, when you stop to think about it, God has given you more blessings than you can count. So the question of the day is this: will you thank Him . . . or not?

God's Word makes it clear: A wise heart is a thankful heart. Period. Yet sometimes, in the crush of everyday living, we simply don't stop long enough to pause and thank our Creator for His blessings. When we neglect God, we suffer. Our Heavenly Father has blessed us beyond measure, and we owe Him *everything*, including our thanks, starting now.

Think About It

No duty is more urgent than
that of returning thanks.
St. Ambrose

The words "thank" and "think" come from
the same root word. If we would
think more, we would thank more.
Warren Wiersbe

Gratitude to God makes even
a temporal blessing a taste of heaven.
William Romaine

Gratitude changes the pangs of memory
into a tranquil joy.
Dietrich Bonhoeffer

THANKSGIVING DAY BY DAY

Q: If life is a celebration, why don't I feel like celebrating?

A: Perhaps all you need is an attitude adjustment: if so, start focusing more on the donut and less on the hole. But if you're feeling *really* sad or deeply depressed, TALK ABOUT IT with people who can help, starting with your parents. If you have persistent feelings of sadness of despair—or if you know somebody who does—seek help immediately. It might be depression, a condition that's both serious and treatable. So don't delay.

A Prayer for Today

Dear Lord, today, I will join in the celebration of life. I will be a joyful Christian, and I will share my joy with all those who cross my path. You have given me countless blessings, Lord, and today I will thank You by celebrating my life, my faith, and my Savior. Amen

For God So Loved the World

For God loved the world in this way:
He gave His only Son, so that everyone
who believes in Him will not perish
but have eternal life.

John 3:16 HCSB

How much does God love you? As long as you're alive, you'll never be able to figure it out because God's love is just too big to comprehend. But this much we know: God loves you so much that He sent His Son, Jesus to come to this earth and to die for you! And, when you accepted Jesus into your heart, God gave you a gift that is more precious than gold: the gift of eternal life.

God's love is bigger and more powerful than anybody can imagine, but His love is *very* real. So do yourself a favor right now: accept God's love with open arms and welcome His Son, Jesus into your heart. When you do, your life will be changed today, tomorrow, and forever.

Think About It

The life of faith is a daily exploration of
the constant and countless ways in which
God's grace and love are experienced.
Eugene Peterson

God's free forgiving love is
the sole source of salvation.
Gerhardus Vos

Love so amazing, so divine,
demands my soul, my life, my all.
Isaac Watts

God has pursued us from farther
than space and longer than time.
John Eldredge

FOR GOD SO LOVED THE WORLD

Q: When should I start getting ready to die?

A: Face it: death is a fact of life, and nobody knows when or where it's going to happen. So when it comes to making plans for life here on earth *and* for life eternal, you'd better be ready to live—*and* to die—right now.

A Prayer for Today

Lord, I'm only here on earth for a brief visit. Heaven is my real home. You've given me the gift of eternal life through Your Son Jesus. I accept Your gift, Lord. And I'll share Your Good News so that others, too, might come to know Christ's healing touch. Amen

Walkin' With the Son

Whoever serves me must follow me.
Then my servant will be with me
everywhere I am. My Father
will honor anyone who serves me.

John 12:26 NCV

Who are you going to walk with today? Are you going to walk with people who worship the ways of the world? Or are you going to walk with the Son of God? Jesus walks with you. Are you walking with Him? Hopefully, you will choose to walk with Him today and every day of your life.

Today provides another glorious opportunity to place yourself in the service of the One from Galilee. May you seek His will, may you trust His word, and may you walk in His footsteps—now and forever—amen.

Think About It

As a child of God, rest in the knowledge
that your Savior precedes you, and
He will walk with you through
each experience of your life.
Henry Blackaby

Teach a man a rule and you help him solve
a problem; teach a man to walk with God
and you help him solve the rest of his life.
John Eldredge

Happiness is the byproduct of a life that
is lived in the will of God. When we
humbly serve others, walk in God's path
of holiness, and do what He tells us,
then we will enjoy happiness.
Warren Wiersbe

WALKIN' WITH THE SON

And One More Thing . . .

When we truly walk with God
throughout our day,
life slowly starts to fall into place.
Bill Hybels

A Prayer for Today

Dear Lord, You sent Your Son so that I might have abundant life and eternal life. Thank You, Father, for my Savior, Christ Jesus. I will follow Him, honor Him, and share His Good News, this day and every day. Amen

More Good Stuff

Quotations and Bible Verses by Topic

Courage

The Lord is my light and my salvation—
so why should I be afraid?
The Lord protects me from danger—
so why should I tremble?
Psalm 27:1 NLT

Take courage.
We walk in the wilderness today
and in the Promised Land tomorrow.
D. L. Moody

When once we are assured that
God is good, then there can be
nothing left to fear.
Hannah Whitall Smith

Strength

I can do all things through Christ
who strengthens me.
Philippians 4:13 NKJV

God is great and God is powerful,
but we must invite him to be powerful in our
lives. His strength is always there, but it's up
to us to provide a channel through which
that power can flow.
Bill Hybels

God is the One who provides our strength,
not only to cope with the demands of
the day, but also to rise above them.
May we look to Him for the strength to soar.
Jim Gallery

MORE GOOD STUFF

Hope

But I will always have hope
and will praise you more and more.
Psalm 71:14 NCV

And because we know Christ is alive,
we have hope for the present
and hope for life beyond the grave.
Billy Graham

The popular idea of faith is of
a certain obstinate optimism: the hope,
tenaciously held in the face of trouble,
that the universe is fundamentally friendly
and things may get better.
J. I. Packer

Tough Times

We also have joy with our troubles,
because we know that these troubles
produce patience. And patience produces
character, and character produces hope.
Romans 5:3,4 NCV

Don't let circumstances distress you.
Rather, look for the will of God
for your life to be revealed in
and through those circumstances.
Billy Graham

No faith is so precious as that
which triumphs over adversity.
C. H. Spurgeon

MORE GOOD STUFF

Prayer

When a believing person prays,
great things happen.
James 5:16 NCV

Prayer is not a work that can be allocated
to one or another group in the church. It
is everybody's responsibility;
it is everybody's privilege.
A. W. Tozer

Prayer moves the arm that moves
the world.
Annie Armstrong

He who kneels most stands best.
D. L. Moody

2 MINUTES A DAY

Kindness

Kind people do themselves a favor,
but cruel people bring trouble
on themselves.
Proverbs 11:17 NCV

If we have the true love of God in
our hearts, we will show it in our lives.
We will not have to go up and down
the earth proclaiming it. We will show it
in everything we say or do.
D. L. Moody

The mark of a Christian is that he will walk
the second mile and turn the other cheek.
A wise man or woman gives
the extra effort, all for the glory of
the Lord Jesus Christ.
John Maxwell

MORE GOOD STUFF

Doing the Right Thing

So don't get tired of doing what is good.
Don't get discouraged and give up,
for we will reap a harvest of blessing
at the appropriate time.
Galatians 6:9 NLT

It may be said without qualification
that every man is as holy and as full of
the Spirit as he wants to be. He may not
be as full as he wishes he were, but he is
most certainly as full as he wants to be.
A. W. Tozer

Learning God's truth and getting it into
our heads is one thing, but *living* God's
truth and getting it into our characters is
quite something else.
Warren Wiersbe

2 MINUTES A DAY

God's Protection

God is our protection and our strength.
He always helps in times of trouble.
Psalm 46:1 NCV

God delights in spreading His protective
wings and enfolding His frightened, weary,
beaten-down, worn-out children.
Bill Hybels

Worries carry responsibilities that belong
to God, not to you. Worry does not
enable us to escape evil; it makes us
unfit to cope with it when it comes.
Corrie ten Boom

MORE GOOD STUFF

Obedience to God

For it is not merely knowing the law
that brings God's approval.
Those who obey the law will be
declared right in God's sight.
Romans 2:13 NLT

Obedience is the outward expression
of your love of God.
Henry Blackaby

All true knowledge of God is born out
of obedience.
John Calvin

God's mark is on everything
that obeys Him.
Martin Luther

Wisdom

Don't depend on your own wisdom.
Respect the Lord and refuse to do wrong.
Proverbs 3:7 NCV

Knowledge is horizontal. Wisdom is vertical;
it comes down from above.
Billy Graham

God's plan for our guidance is for us
to grow gradually in wisdom
before we get to the crossroads.
Bill Hybels

The fruit of wisdom is Christlikeness, peace,
humility, and love. And, the root of it is faith
in Christ as the manifested wisdom of God.
J. I. Packer

MORE GOOD STUFF

Faith

Anything is possible if a person believes.
Mark 9:23 NLT

We have a God who delights in
impossibilities.
Andrew Murray

How do you walk in faith?
By claiming the promises of God
and obeying the Word of God,
in spite of what you see, how you feel,
or what may happen.
Warren Wiersbe

Faith means believing in advance what
will only make sense in reverse.
Philip Yancey

The Past

The Lord says, "Forget what happened
before, and do not think about the past.
Look at the new thing I am going to do.
It is already happening."
Isaiah 43:18,19 ncv

The devil keeps so many of us stuck in
our weakness. He reminds us of our pasts
when we ought to remind him of
his future—he doesn't have one.
Franklin Graham

Leave the broken, irreversible past
in God's hands, and step out into
the invincible future with Him.
Oswald Chambers

God forgets the past. Imitate him.
Max Lucado

MORE GOOD STUFF

his devotional

Doing It Now

Do what God's teaching says;
when you only listen and do nothing,
you are fooling yourselves.
James 1:22 NCV

Give to us clear vision that we may know
where to stand and what to stand for.
Let us not be content to wait and
see what will happen, but give us
the determination to make
the right things happen.
Peter Marshall

He who waits until circumstances
completely favor his undertaking
will never accomplish anything.
Martin Luther

2 MINUTES A DAY

Anger

Foolish people are always fighting, but avoiding quarrels will bring you honor.
Proverbs 20:3 ncv

Anger is a kind of temporary madness.
St. Basil the Great

Bitterness and anger, usually over trivial things, make havoc of homes, churches, and friendships.
Warren Wiersbe

What is hatred, after all, other than anger that was allowed to remain, that has become ingrained and deep-rooted? What was anger when it was fresh becomes hatred when it is aged.
St. Augustine

MORE GOOD STUFF

Attitude

Finally brothers, whatever is true,
whatever is honorable, whatever is just,
whatever is pure, whatever is lovely,
whatever is commendable—if there is any
moral excellence and if there is
any praise—dwell on these things.
Philippians 4:8 HCSB

Attitude is more important than
the past, than education, than money,
than circumstances, than what people
do or say. It is more important than
appearance, giftedness, or skill.
Charles Swindoll

Don't believe in defeat.
Norman Vincent Peale

Forgiveness

Don't pick on people, jump on their
failures, criticize their faults—unless,
of course, you want the same treatment.
Don't condemn those who are down;
that hardness can boomerang. Be easy
on people; you'll find life a lot easier.
Luke 6:37 MSG

I firmly believe a great many prayers
are not answered because
we are not willing to forgive someone.
D. L. Moody

Forgiveness is not an emotion.
Forgiveness is an act of the will,
and the will can function regardless of
the temperature of the heart.
Corrie ten Boom

MORE GOOD STUFF

God's Word

But He answered, "It is written:
Man must not live on bread alone,
but on every word that comes
from the mouth of God."
Matthew 4:4 HCSB

God has given us all sorts of counsel
and direction in his written Word;
thank God, we have it written down
in black and white.
John Eldredge

Prayer and the Word are inseparably
linked together. Power in the use of either
depends on the presence of the other.
Andrew Murray

2 MINUTES A DAY

Asking God

Ask, and God will give to you. Search,
and you will find. Knock, and the door
will open for you. Yes, everyone who asks
will receive. Everyone who searches
will find. And everyone who knocks
will have the door opened.
Matthew 7:7,8 NCV

When you ask God to do something,
don't ask timidly;
put your whole heart into it.
Marie T. Freeman

God will help us become the people we
are meant to be, if only we will ask Him.
Hannah Whitall Smith

MORE GOOD STUFF

God's Love

The unfailing love of the Lord never ends!
Lamentations 3:22 NLT

The hope we have in Jesus is
the anchor for the soul—something sure
and steadfast, preventing drifting or giving
way, lowered to the depth of God's love.
Franklin Graham

If God had a refrigerator, your picture
would be on it. If he had a wallet,
your photo would be in it. He sends
you flowers every spring
and a sunrise every morning.
Max Lucado

2 MINUTES A DAY